All Hair is Good Hair

ANNAGJID KEE TAYLOR

AuthorHouse™
1663 Liberty Drive
Bloomington, IN 47403
www.authorhouse.com
Phone: 1 (800) 839-8640

This book is printed on acid-free paper.

ISBN: 978-1-7283-3190-4 (sc)
ISBN: 978-1-7283-3192-8 (hc)
ISBN: 978-1-7283-3191-1 (e)

Library of Congress Control Number: 2019916375

Print information available on the last page.

Published by AuthorHouse 11/27/2019

authorHOUSE

This is dedicated to my mommy,
Juanda Taylor-Walston also known as "Yasmeen"
who's two favorite things in this life were children and hair.

About The Author

Annagjid "Kee" Taylor, who got her start in her parent's basement is now a CEO, Innovator, Deeper Than Hair salon owner and Hairstylist. As a celebrity hairstylist she often travels from city to city working in film and television. Her advanced haircare line Shear Genius Collection as well as her artistic hair skills have been published on digital platforms as well as print magazines such as O, The Oprah Magazine, Essence, InStyle Romania and Sheen. Her internet breaking hair styles can be found on red carpets as well as her YouTube channel, Deeper Than Hair TV. When Kee is not on set she can be found educating other hairstylists via Deeper Than Hair University and in major cities for pop-up salon visits.

Even though Kee works with celebrities, all of her clients are equally important. She wants to make sure everyone understands the importance of embracing your natural God given tresses! With experience in early childhood education, she believes it's most effective to start with children.

In her first children's book, ALL HAIR IS GOOD HAIR, she shares how early hair experiences gives rise to the revolutionary vision of hair freedom and empowerment.

"My name is _____ and ALL hair is good hair!"

Why can't my hair be like Dominique's? It's so long and straight. I wish my hair was good like hers.

"STOP! My mom said nobody is allowed to play in my hair." yelled Samaya as three of her classmates reach out and touch her hair.

"Why does it feel like that?" Anna teased.

"It's so short and rough," Veen joked.

"Yeah, haha, it feels just like a rug!" giggled Ashley.

"Hurry, put your seatbelt on, you know you have a doctor's appointment today," said Samaya's mom.

"I hate school! I never want to come here again!" yelled Samaya.

"What?! What happened?" her mother asked in concern.

"Mommy, why don't I have GOOD hair? I hate that my hair is BAD!" Samaya cried.

"Baby, who told you your hair was bad? There is no such thing as bad hair. ALL hair is good hair as long as it's healthy!" replied Samaya's mom almost in tears herself.

"Really, why don't you wear your hair like mine?" asked Samaya.

"Well..." she paused. "I don't know. My mother relaxed my hair when I was your age and I never changed it. Plus it's easier for mommy," she replied.

"Please Mom, can I get it done at the salon like yours?" she begged.

"Your hair is PERFECT just the way it is. Of course you can straighten it every now and again but only if it's for YOUR happiness and no one else's. I will make you an appointment." answered her mom.

"Ok, Samaya. Everything looked good today, including your hair!" said Dr. Tah.

Samaya dropped her head.

"What's wrong?" her doctor asked.

"It's just that I don't really like my bad hair," she replied.

"Oh, I see. Well, I think your hair is wonderful! Think about it. You can wear it any way you want. Up, down, curly, twists, straight, in a bun or even braided. If that's not GOOD hair, I dont know what is!"

"You look beautiful today, Samaya."

"You're just saying that cause you're my mommy," she replied with her head still down in sadness.

"Remember what I said. ALL hair is good hair and don't let anyone tell you different. Have a great day today!"

"Good Afternoon, Principal Wright. My teacher asked me to bring this down to you."

"Thank you so much, young lady. I really like your hair by the way!" said Principal Wright.

"Thanks." Samaya replied with a slight smile.

"Are you ok?" asked Principal Wright.

"Well, it's just that I don't like my hair and neither does any of my friends. I don't have good hair like they do. In two more days I get to change it!" she said.

"Think about this: Your hair is beautiful and was created just for you. As long as YOU love it, nothing else matters. It is a gift and a treasure. If that's not GOOD hair, I don't know what is!"

"Hey girlfriend! Your hair is so cute! I gotta try that one day!" said the bank teller.

"Thank you, I guess." Samaya answered

"What's the matter?"

"I have bad hair. it's nothing like my mom's or anyone that I know." said Samaya.

"Think about it! Your hair is unique. It makes you stand out from the crowd and makes you special in your very OWN way! If we all were the same that wouldn't be fun, now would it? If that's not GOOD hair, I don't know what is!"

"Happy Saturday, Samaya! Our hair appointment is at 10:30."

"Mom, I've been thinking and I have decided to keep my hair just the way it is. You were right. It isn't bad. My hair IS good! I tried some styles this week and I'm starting to love my hair now!" Samaya said proudly.

"Aww baby! I'm so proud of you! Well you can stay home with daddy and I'll see you when I get back from getting my hair done!"

"I'm sorry for staring but I really love your hair. I wish my daughter could have been here to see it." said Samaya's mom in frustration.

"Really, why?" asked the woman.

"She has been sad lately because she thinks she has bad hair, so I love when she can see women with hair just like hers."

"Aww," the woman replied. "Just let her know that her hair is the CROWN that she will never take off! If that's not GOOD hair I don't know what is!"

"SAMAYA, IM HOME! TIME FOR DINNER!"

"COMING!" she yelled while running down the stairs.

"MOM!! YOU CUT YOUR HAIR?!!" Samaya yells in complete shock.

"Yup, I sure did." said her mom with her head held high.

"But...but, why?!" said Samaya, still in disbelief.

"Well honey, I figured this is a journey that we both can take... together."

Then Samaya replied, "If thats not GOOD hair, I don't know what is."

The End

Printed in the United States
By Bookmasters